#6

The Crazy
Classroom Caper

Don't Miss

#6

The Crazy Classroom Caper

BY

Tony Abbott

ILLUSTRATED BY

Colleen Madden

EGMONT
New York   USA

EGMONT

We bring stories to life

First published by Egmont USA, 2014
443 Park Avenue South, Suite 806
New York, NY 10016

Text copyright © Tony Abbott, 2014
Illustrations copyright © Colleen Madden, 2014
All rights reserved

1 3 5 7 9 8 6 4 2

www.egmontusa.com
www.tonyabbottbooks.com
www.greenfrographics.com

Library of Congress Cataloging-in-Publication Data
Abbott, Tony, 1952-
The crazy classroom caper / by Tony Abbott;
illustrated by Colleen Madden.
pages cm. — (Goofballs ; #6)
Summary: When objects go missing in a kindergarten classroom,
the Goofballs go undercover as teachers to crack the case.
ISBN 978-1-60684-449-6 (hardback) — ISBN 978-1-60684-450-2
(digest paperback) [1. Mystery and detective stories. 2. Schools —
Fiction. 3. Teachers — Fiction. 4. Lost and found possessions — Fiction.
5. Humorous stories.] I. Madden, Colleen, illustrator. II. Title.
PZ7.A1587Ct 2014
[Fic] — dc23
2013018254

Printed in the United States of America

Book design by Kathleen Westray

To Goofballs everywhere

(You know who you are!)

Contents

1

The Mysterious Mitten-Sock

I'm Jeff Bunter, and I'm a Goofball.

That's spelled G-O-O-F-B-A-L-L.

I've been spelling lots of words lately. Like D-O-G and C-A-T and S-T-O-P—I-T!

That's because yesterday I was not only a Goofball, I was also a T-E-A-C-H-E-R.

There was a really hard mystery in Miss Becker's kindergarten classroom, and the Goofballs went undercover as teachers to solve it.

But we almost didn't solve it.

In fact, we almost F-A-I-L-E-D!

Luckily, four Goofballs plus one Goofdog equal one pretty okay teacher.

Brian Rooney is a world-class almost celebrity inventor of goofy inventions that don't really work, but he knows all about science and math like it's his job.

Mara Lubin is a genius of disguises. Plus she's as skinny as a pencil and knows how to use one to draw pictures that look like real art.

Kelly Smitts knows history, is super smart, super serious, and super smart. I said "smart" twice because she's *that* smart. But she's also super goofy. She has to be, or she wouldn't hang out with the rest of us.

I'm a detective from my toes to my nose. I see clues everywhere, and I write them all down in my handy cluebook.

Finally, there's Sparky, my corgi. He graduated obedience school with the highest marks in the class, even though his short legs made him the lowest dog in the class.

Plus he barks like this: "Goof! Goof!"

But even when you add up all that incredible detective talent, this case was nearly our L-A-S-T!

It started two days ago during final period.

Mara and I were sitting at our usual table in the cafeteria, waiting for Brian and Kelly.

We had a free period, which is exactly like having no case, which is exactly what we were talking about.

"We haven't solved a mystery in days," Mara said with a sigh. "I think I'm forgetting what a clue looks like."

"Me, too," I grumbled. "Is that a clue?"

I pointed at a man in overalls and a pink cap carrying a ladder and a can of paint.

Mara frowned. "No. He's just a guy."

"He's not just a guy. He's Daddy!"

We turned to see Violet Boggs standing behind us with her tiny sister, Scarlet.

Violet means purple, but she always wears pink. *Scarlet* means red, but she always wears green.

"We have a free period, too," said Violet.

"It better be free," said Scarlet. "We just spent our last quarter on trail mix."

"Why is your dad here?" I asked, getting ready to write the answer in my cluebook.

"Badger Point Elementary is an old school," Violet said. "And Daddy's helping build new kindergarten classrooms upstairs. Last week he found a weird old elevator."

"And he took it!" said Scarlet.
"Took. Spelled K-O-O-T!"

"Um . . . T-O-O-K," Violet said to
her sister.

"Your father took the elevator?" said Mara. "Where did he take it?"

"Out!" said Scarlet. "Spelled O-W-W-T."

"That's really spelled O-U-T," Violet said. "Which is where we need to go now. Bye!"

As they both ran to catch up to their father, I wrote it all in my cluebook.

Mr. Boggs
Elevator
K-O-O-T = TOOK
O-W-W-T = OUT

Mara sighed again. "You can write it down, but that doesn't make it a mystery."

"I guess that's true," I said.

"You even know what I did this morning?" she said. "I tried hiding my own shoes and forgetting where they were so I could search for them."

"Did it work?" I asked.

She shook her head. "No. My mind told me right where they were."

"My mind tells me stuff all the time," said Brian, who was zigzagging his way between the tables to us. "But I surprise it by not listening."

I was going to write that down, too. But there was no mystery about it.

Brian often doesn't listen to his mind.

"That's fairly goofy," I said.

"You know what's goofy?" Kelly said as she powerwalked over to us, her arms swinging and her mouth laughing.

"I just saw Scarlet Boggs for the second time today. This morning, she ran out of Miss Becker's kindergarten class to give Principal Higgins a scribbled note."

Miss Becker was our old kindergarten teacher, but she wasn't old. She was young and fun and the greatest teacher ever.

When we were small, Brian and I had her for a.m. kindergarten, and Kelly and Mara had her for p.m. Now kindergarten is all day long.

"Principal Higgins turned Scarlet's note one way," Kelly said. "Then the other way. Then upside down. Finally, he said, 'Wonderful! I love it!' Guys, you should have seen his face!"

"I've seen it before," said Brian. "I'm sure I would recognize it."

I wrote it all down.

Scarlet's note to Principal Higgins
"Wonderful! I love it!"
His face

"I miss Miss Becker," Mara said. "It was so easy to find a mystery in kindergarten."

I swung around and looked at Brian. He swung around and looked at me.

"The Mystery of the Missing Mitten and the Missing Sock!" we both said together.

Mara jumped. "Tell us!"

"Well," I said, "it was our first case in Miss Becker's class. Brian and I shared a cubby. One day, I pulled on my dark blue mittens, and Brian pulled on his dark blue socks."

"Stop right there," said Kelly. "Brian, why weren't you wearing socks in class?"

"I like to feel the carpet under my toes," he said. "Miss Becker has the best carpet."

"She really does," I added.

"Then what happened?" Mara asked.

"One mitten was fine," I said. "But as soon as I pulled on my other mitten, I realized that someone had stolen the thumb from it!"

Brian gasped. "Not only that. The thief had attached the thumb to one of my socks!"

Kelly frowned. "Wait. Weren't they just mixed —"

"Shh!" said Brian. "We're telling it."

I nodded. "As Goofballs, we knew that a criminal always returns to the scene of the crime."

"So we put the wrong mitten and the wrong sock back in the cubby and waited in the closet for the thief to return," said Brian.

"A stakeout!" said Mara. "Then what happened?"

Brian sighed. "I fell asleep on the job. Which I'd never do now."

"And because I had no one to talk to, I fell asleep, too," I said.

"When we woke up," said Brian, "both the mitten and the sock had vanished."

"So when I left school, I kept one hand in my pocket," I said.

"And I hopped all the way home," Brian said. "But whoever did it is still out there."

"I think you two are out there," said Kelly.

"I have an idea," said Mara. "Let's see if Miss Becker remembers us!"

Before you could spell Y-E-S, we were racing through the halls to K wing.

"She'll be so happy to see us!" I said.

But when we got to her classroom, Miss Becker wasn't happy.

She wasn't happy at all.

When she came to the door, she frowned and sighed and wiped a tear from her cheek and said, "Goofballs, something is very wrong!"

2

The Disappearing Classroom

"What's the matter?" asked Kelly.

Miss Becker closed the classroom door behind her, stood in the hall with us, and leaned close.

"Something's happening in my classroom. Something very . . . oh, what's the word—"

Brian raised his hand. "Elephant."

"No, no—"

"Spaceship?"

"No, Brian—"

"Nutcracker!"

"Please—"

"Garbonzo beans! My final answer."

Miss Becker shook her head. "What I was going to say is that something very *mysterious* is happening in my classroom."

"I'm practically choking on my own breath!" said Mara, fanning her face.

"What she means," said Brian, "is that we *solve* mysteries. We're the Goofballs."

"I know that, of course," Miss Becker said. "The mitten and the sock."

"I hopped all the way home," said Brian.

"I know," Miss B. said. "I watched you."

"Ahem," said Kelly. "Getting back to the mystery . . ."

Miss Becker pointed through the window on the door. "Tomorrow is our last day in this room."

"We heard about that," said Mara. "You're moving up to a new classroom, aren't you?"

Miss Becker nodded. "But I'll miss this one and everything in it. I call it my Wonderland, because so many wonderful things happen here."

"They do," said Brian. "I'm living proof."

"The reading tree," she said, "the tiny fish tank, the squeaky rocking chair, the lopsided bookshelf, the old cardboard puppet theater. I'll miss them all."

"Life is about change," said Kelly. "You taught us that. So turn that frown upside down. Make it a smiley face. Just like you taught us on the art easel."

"I drew my first circle on that easel," Mara said. "It was the beginning of my career as an artist and a fashion person."

"That's just it," Miss Becker said. "That same easel — my old high school art easel — has just vanished!"

I gasped. "That's terrible!"

"Or magical!" said Mara.

Miss Becker frowned even more. "This morning some pencils went missing. Then a tub of building blocks. Just before lunch — *poof!* — all the crayons disappeared!"

"So the kids really are magicians?" said Mara.

"Or aliens beaming stuff up to the mother ship?" Brian asked.

"Or just plain bad?" I asked.

"No, no, and no," said Miss Becker. "The kids are wonderful. They've known for a while that we'll be leaving this room, but it really hit me yesterday how much I'll miss it. It was my first classroom. . . ."

"Aha!" said Mara.

"Did you solve the mystery?" I asked.

"No. Just practicing for when I do."

"Well," Miss Becker said, "ever since this morning, things have been vanishing. I can't explain it. The kids say they have no idea."

Miss Becker opened the door. The kids were sitting together on the floor. Their eyes were focused on Miss Becker. Their beaming faces told me that they loved her just like we did.

So *why* were things vanishing from Miss Becker's Wonderland?

And, maybe more important, *how*?

"Miss Becker," I said, "I have an idea that's so good I could say it a hundred times. But I won't. But I could. The Goofballs will solve the mystery of your disappearing stuff. Because the Goofballs will go undercover to teach your class!"

"Yes!" said Mara. "We'll disguise ourselves as teachers and find out the truth!"

"Teachers love the truth," said Kelly.

"T-R-U-T-H," said Brian. "Look, I'm starting already."

Miss Becker tapped her chin as if she was thinking it over. "I don't know. I *could* use a day off. But this class is a real handful."

"That's okay," I said. "All together, the Goofballs have eight hands and four paws!"

She smiled. "If Principal Higgins and your teacher, Mrs. Lang, say you can, then yes. Now, excuse me, I must go back in."

As soon as she closed the door, Principal Higgins trotted down the hall, shuffling his papers and plans, followed by Mr. Boggs, the builder.

Principal Higgins shook his head. "I can't believe there's a room in my school that I never heard of! Why is there an extra room?"

"It's where the elevator was," Mr. Boggs said.

Kelly turned to us, grinning like the winner of a grinning contest. "Let me handle this."

She planted herself in the hallway right in front of the principal.

"Principal Higgins!" she said.

He screeched to a stop. "Yes, Kelly?"

"Miss Becker is great, isn't she?" she asked.

He blinked. "Why, yes, of course she is!"

"Do you think we could be teachers like Miss Becker one day?" Kelly asked.

"Absolutely!" he said. "That would be excellent. You'd be great teachers. Now excuse me. There's still so much work to do!"

Principal Higgins shot to the end of the hall and screeched around the corner.

"How will that help us?" Mara asked.

Kelly kept her grin going. "Principal Higgins said we could be teachers one day. What he doesn't know is that that day . . . is tomorrow!"

"Very S-M-A-R-T," said Brian.

"Thank you," said Kelly.

That's when Miss Becker leaned out her classroom door and said, "Better hurry and solve our mystery. While I was talking to you, our little puppet theater vanished!"

3

How to Get Smart

"Goofballs," I said, "we've got ourselves an awesome new mystery."

We ran right away to our teacher, Mrs. Lang, and told her our plan. She agreed, then added, "I used to teach kindergarten, you know."

"Do you have any advice?" asked Mara.

"Get a good night's sleep tonight," Mrs. Lang said with a sigh. "You'll need it."

When we left the classroom, Kelly said, "There's only one real way to pretend to be as smart as undercover teachers—"

Brian held up his hand. "Don't say it. I knew you'd ask me to teach you everything I know. Sorry, I can't."

"Why not?" I asked. "Because what you know is so scary?"

"Because what you know would make us nuts?" asked Kelly.

"Because our brains would throw up?" asked Mara.

"No, no, and maybe," said Brian, "it's because my brain is so huge, the government has classified it. It's a secret. Even from me."

"That explains so much," I said.

"Exactly," said Brian. "My brain is so big, it's hard for me *not* to explain so much."

Kelly grumbled. "The *real* best place to learn is the school library. Follow me."

"M-E," Brian said. "I am so good at this."

We marched upstairs to the second floor. There were workmen crawling everywhere, pounding, sawing, painting, trying to finish the new classrooms in only one more day.

I wrote that down in my cluebook because you never know if something means something until it means it. Which sounded good, so I wrote that down, too.

You never know if something means something until it means it.

When we got to the library, the door was shut tight.

"The library is never closed," said Kelly.

We knocked.

We knocked again.

We knocked again again.

The door opened a crack. Mr. Silver, the librarian, popped out his head. "Hello?"

"Our free period's half over and we need to learn stuff," said Brian.

"Slide in," he said. After we slid in one by one, he closed the door tightly behind us.

"I'm keeping the door closed because of all the dust from the construction," he said. "Look." Then he shook his head, and a shower of white dust fell onto his shoes.

"Now, how can I help you?" he asked.

"We need to know everything teachers know," said Mara. "We have . . . a half hour."

Mr. Silver blinked. "I see. Well, the best way to do that is for each of you to pick a favorite subject. What do you like to do?"

"Art," said Mara. "Because I draw very well, and art is where fashion comes from, and I do fashion very well, too."

"I'd be so great at art," said Brian.

"But I don't want to be right now."

"I'll take history," said Kelly.

"I know so much history!" Brian groaned. "Right now I'm thinking of bananas, and the last banana I had was this morning. That's historical."

"You're bananas," Kelly said. "*I'm* doing history."

I looked at the shelves stretching to the back of the room. "Reading and writing for me."

"I was going to do those!" said Brian. "But I could never figure out which came first, reading or writing."

"Really?" said Mr. Silver.

"Think about it," Brian said. "Reading couldn't come before writing because there would be nothing to read. But writing couldn't come before reading because writers couldn't read what they wrote."

We all stared at him.

"It's a riddle," Brian said.

"So are you," said Kelly.

"Why not take math and science?" asked Mr. Silver.

Brian beamed. "Yes! I'm already an almost world-class celebrity inventor of inventions."

So for the next thirty minutes, we read books and wrote notes and made pictures and looked up stuff and looked down stuff and looked at stuff from every angle.

The library wasn't as quiet as it normally is. The workmen kept up their noises the entire time.

"All that drilling and pounding and banging is making my brain want to explode," Mr. Silver said.

"My brain wants to explode right now," Brian said, "but the government won't let it."

We were so deep in studying that we almost didn't hear the bell ring, but by the end of the afternoon, the four of us equaled one pretty good teacher.

"Goofball mystery solvers," I said, "tomorrow morning at nine sharp, we report for duty in room Four-K."

"Our first day as undercover teachers," said Mara. "I can't wait."

"Our students will be so smart by the end of the day," said Kelly, "Principal Higgins won't even believe it."

Brian grumbled. "I already don't believe it. I'm starting to forget everything I just read!"

4

Where in the World?

When we met in classroom 4K the next morning, we looked just like real teachers.

My hair was combed neatly, and I wore the suit Grandma gave me, including a necktie, a vest, and shiny shoes.

I didn't even look like me.

Kelly wore a brown sweater, a brown dress, and brown shoes. She couldn't do her normal powerwalk because her arms were weighed down with books and papers.

Mara wore a lady dress and shoes with high heels on them. They made her even taller than normal, so that the pencils sticking out of her hair nearly scraped the ceiling.

Brian zoomed in wearing baggy pants and a rumpled sport coat. His pockets bulged with invention junk, his hair was all crazy, and a furry thing was hanging over his mouth.

"Sorry I'm late," he said. "I had to grow this mustache. Call me Professor Shmartz! Math wiz and inventor of inventions!"

Finally, Sparky trotted in, wearing a little graduation hat, and the kids went crazy.

They cheered and jumped from their seats and crowded around him.

"Settle down, class," Kelly said.

"Miss B. will be out today," I told the students, "so we'll be your teachers. First things first, let's take attendance."

"Take it where?" said one boy.

The kids laughed.

I tapped my cluebook. "We want to see if everyone is here."

"I'm here," said a boy with red hair.

"Me, too!" said the girl next to him.

The class laughed more.

"Save yourself some time," a grouchy little boy said. "We're *all* here!"

The class laughed the most.

"Tough crowd," Brian whispered under his mustache.

I finally got all their names down.

Mara used one of her pencils to draw faces next to the names so we'd remember them.

"Now it's time for history," said Kelly, setting her papers on the desk. "Today our lesson will be all about—"

The girl named Julie raised her hand.

"Yes?" Kelly said.

"I . . . to . . . now . . . ," Julie whispered.

"I'm sorry, what did you say?" Kelly asked.

Julie ran up to her. "I said I have to throw up now."

And she did, all over Kelly's papers.

"Agggg!" Kelly yelled.

Then Julie ran straight to the bathroom.

Kelly staggered back from her pukey notes. "If only she went to the bathroom first."

"I'll take over," said Brian, moving to the front of the class. *"Zip! Bing! Plink—"*

"Hey!" snarled Lil Mikey, the grumpy kid from before. "What's that noise?"

"That, son, is my math and science brain," Brian said under his mustache. Then he spun the globe. "Let Professor Shmartz give you a tour of our world!"

"Oh, yeah?" Mikey growled. "Well, zippety-plinkety-boo. I already know where every country in the world is. Ask me."

Brian frowned. "My lesson isn't—"

"I said, *ask me*!" said Lil Mikey.

"Ask him! Ask him!" the kids cheered.

"These kids are a handful, all right," Mara whispered.

I kept my eye on all the stuff in the classroom. I was determined that nothing would go missing today. So far so good.

Brian leaned over to the globe. "Let me see. All right. Tell me where France is."

Lil Mikey stood up. "The same place it was last year!"

The kids laughed.

"But where's that?" Brian asked.

"Right where it should be!"

The kids laughed harder.

"I mean, where is it located?"

"Where nothing else is!" Lil Mikey said, and the kids fell on the floor, laughing.

Brian seemed dazed as he plopped into Miss Becker's rocking chair. "What just happened?"

"You've been outgoofed," said Mara. "Let me try. Good teachers make work seem fun."

She clacked her heels together loudly, and all the kids looked up at her.

"Does everyone like art?" she asked.

"Yes!" they cried.

"Does everyone like math?"

"No!" they cried.

"Then let's do ArtMath!" she said.

"Yay!" they cheered.

Mara then picked up a piece of chalk and drew really fancy numbers on the chalkboard.

Kathy's hand shot up and so did the rest of her. "Two plus two plus two equals *one*!"

Mara frowned. "How can two plus two plus two equal *one*?"

"Two eyes, two ears, and two lips equal *one* face!" Kathy said.

"Yay, ArtMath!" everyone cheered.

Suddenly, Langston screamed at the top of his lungs. "Where's Sprinkle?"

"Sprinkle?" I said. "You mean Sparky?" I pointed behind me. "He's right here."

"Goof?" said Sparky.

"No! Sprinkle!" said Langston. "Our fish. The fish tank is gone! Oh, poor Sprinkle!"

Scarlet jumped from her seat and whispered in Langston's ear.

"Oh, I forgot," he said. "Never mind."

Kelly jumped to the windowsill. "Where *is* the fish tank? How could it just vanish? We were all right here."

"Here?" said Truman, the red-haired boy. "Are we taking attendance again? Because I'm pretty sure I'm still here."

"Me, too!" said Julie, back from the bathroom and smelling like mint.

My brain went *click*. "Aha! You're *all* here! Which means that every student in this classroom is . . . a witness!"

"Prove it!" said Lil Mikey.

Witness is a special detective word that means *someone who saw something happen*.

I glared down at the students. "So . . . did anyone see anything?"

The girl named Katie twirled in her seat. "I saw a cow once!" she said.

"If you saw it again," said Neal, "that's two cows."

"My daddy has a cow," said Regina. "He dwives it to work evwy day!"

I stared at them. Then I stared at the other Goofballs. Then I stared at the clock.

It was still first period.

"Seriously?" I said. "There are another six hours of this?"

"Only if you don't count naptime," said Kelly.

"But how can fourteen kids seem like so many more?" asked Mara.

"That's kindergarten math," said Brian.

5

The Mystery of History

We decided right then that adding four Goofballs and one Goofdog might not be the way to solve this mystery.

"Guys, we need to do some division," I said. "One of us teaches while the rest of us search for C-L-U-E-S."

"Kelly?" said Mara. "Do you think you can try again?"

"I guess so," she said. "What's the worst that can happen?"

"You probably shouldn't ask that," said Brian.

Kelly swallowed hard and took her place in front of the room. I could see she was still upset by Julie getting sick on her notes.

But a Goofball never quits.

Kelly gave us a nod. When she began to teach, Brian, Mara, Sparky, and I crept slowly around the classroom like hunting dogs. We sniffed and nosed and pawed everything we saw, searching for clues to solve our mystery.

I stalked around the place where the goldfish tank used to be.

Brian went down the aisles, looking for clues to the missing puppet theater.

Mara searched the closets and under the tables for evidence of the missing art easel.

Nothing.

Nothing.

Nothing.

Meanwhile, Kelly wasn't doing much better.

"What can anyone tell me about George Washington?" she asked the class.

"He invented laundry," said the girl named Colleen. "He loved *washing* so much he did a *ton* of it. So they called him *Washing . . . ton*."

Kelly frowned. "Hmm. Anyone else?"

Truman raised his hand. "He lived in Washington, DC, because it had the same name as him, so he always knew when to get off the train."

"That might be a little wrong," Kelly said.

"Of course it's wrong," said Henri. "We all know George Washington never took trains."

"That's right," said Kelly. "And how do we know that?"

"Because Washington *drove* a *car*," Henri said. "That's what DC stands for. *Drove* a *car!*"

Kelly practically choked. "I'm . . . I'm . . . dumbfounded!"

"That's a bad word," Regina said. "I'm telling Miss Becker."

Kelly
started to
wobble, so
we carried
her back
to Miss
Becker's
rocking
chair.

"Teaching is hard," she groaned.

It was about to get even harder.

"My turn," I said, marching to the front of the class. "Kids, I'm going to read you my favorite story. It's about a boy named Noodle and his best friend, Zeek. Gather at the reading tree while I get my book. . . ."

"We can't even do that!" shouted Eric.

"Of course we can," I said. "The tree is right over — *akkkk!* The reading tree is gone!"

"Now we'll never learn to read!" the kids cried. And they started running in circles around where the tree used to be.

"Goof! Goof!" Sparky barked as he chased them around, trying to get them back into their seats.

I swung around to my fellow detectives. "Goofballs!" I cried. "What's going on here? We're losing stuff left and right."

"And in the middle, too," Brian added.

In my cluebook, I put an X next to each thing missing. It wasn't looking good. There were *way* too many Xs!

"Hold on," Kelly whispered. "I bet the tree vanished the moment you helped me to the rocking chair. These kids must be doing it!"

Suddenly, the bell rang.

"Lunchtime!" Regina cried out.

"Run and get your lunches, please," said Mara, and the kids rushed to their cubbies in the back of the room.

"Keep your eyes on those kids," I said. "Don't let any of them out of your sight. . . ."

No sooner had the kids grabbed their lunch bags than they suddenly made a wall completely across the back of the room. "Lunchtime!" they sang. Then they hurried back to their tables and started munching.

"That was weird," said Brian.

"Maybe singing is a new kindergarten tradition," I said, counting the kids one by one as they took their seats. "Eleven, twelve, thirteen . . . thirteen . . ."

I counted the students again. "Thirteen?"

I started to shiver.

Even though we had all the kids in plain sight the whole time, *one of them had just vanished.*

Vanished!

"Um," I said, "where's number fourteen?"

"Right between thirteen and fifteen!" said Kathy.

"Teachers should know their numbers," Leonardo added.

"Teachers should also not lose their students," said Kelly.

6

W-O-N-S = SNOW = AHA!

Now I was worried. Losing a reading tree was one thing. But losing a student? There were probably rules against that.

I immediately checked the room chart. Only one person wasn't there.

"Scarlet Boggs? We lost Scarlet Boggs? Where did she go? And how?"

No one raised a hand. Every
student looked down at his or her
lunch and ate quietly.

Mara clacked her heels again.
"Everyone, stop eating and look up at
me this instant."

They did.

"You know that lying is wrong,
don't you?" she asked.

Regina raised her hand. "No, it's
not. Mommy says I have to lie once
evwy day."

"She does?" I asked.

"She says, 'Lie on your bed and go
to sleep!' I'll do it wight now, see?"

Regina put her head down and
started snoring. Everyone giggled and
kept eating.

"Goofballs!" I whispered, not taking my eyes off the class. "We're getting nowhere!"

"Meanwhile, Scarlet Boggs is getting everywhere," said Kelly. "This is bad."

Suddenly, the knob on the classroom door squeaked. We swung around. When the door opened, Scarlet Boggs walked in. Her thumb was in her mouth. Her other hand was clutching her lunch bag.

"How did you do that?" I asked.

"Do what?" she said around her thumb.

"How did you just *appear* there?" I asked.

She pulled her thumb out and wiped it on her green shirt. "I *appear* wherever I am," she said. "And look. Snow!" She lowered her head and brushed her hair and white dust came flaking off like snow. "Spelled W-O-N-S!"

"Aha!" Kelly gasped. "Worker dust! You left this classroom!"

"I do every day," Scarlet said. "It's how I get home when school's over."

Kelly strode right up to her and set her hands on her hips. "Scarlet, where *exactly* have you been?"

She looked up at Kelly with her big eyes. "Canada, once. New York City, three times. And Florida, where Grammy lives," she said. "But I love Badger Point the best!"

"Yay, Badger Point!" the kids cheered.

"Now I have to eat," said Scarlet.

"Sit! Eat!" Brian said. He swept the snow dust into an evidence bag and stuffed it in his pocket. Then he took out a cardboard tube covered with foil. With an elastic band attached to it, he put it over his head and onto his nose.

"Professor Shmartz will sniff out more evidence. Behold how he moves!" He took slow giant steps from table to table.

I couldn't figure out *how* Scarlet had gone from the back of the classroom to the hallway outside the room while we were all watching.

It was impossible.

Except that she had just done it!

"Professor Shmartz, stop!" Brian yelled out to himself. He stopped. "Something's very fishy in this classroom," he said.

"Not Sprinkle. He's gone," said Langston. "But never mind."

"It's my tuna melt," said Scarlet. "I have to wait for it to cool."

Brian jumped. "Aha and aha! Scarlet, if your lunch has been in the cubby all morning, why is your sandwich so hot?"

"So the cheese can melt, silly!" she said.

"Yay, cheese!" everyone yelled.

Kelly dragged us back to the front of the room. "Goofballs," she whispered, "these kids are up to something, but they're in it together."

"You're right!" I said.

"I say we forget trying to make them spill the beans," Kelly continued. "Let's concentrate on the missing stuff."

"Meaning," said Kelly, "that there are two parts to every disappearance. Part one, something leaves where it is. Part two, it goes somewhere else."

"That makes sense," said Brian.

"Good work, Kelly," I said. "Since we can't seem to stop things from leaving this classroom, we should search for where they've ended up."

Mara grinned. "That's a great detective bit. Write it in your cluebook, Jeff."

I did.

The bell rang again.

"Naptime!" shouted Truman.

Leonardo tapped Regina on the head with a pencil. "Regina, wake up. It's naptime."

I nodded slowly. "Naptime for them is detective time for us."

"Leave Sparky with me," whispered Brian. "We'll check every inch of the classroom while they're napping. You guys search the rest of the school."

"Let's snoop!" said Mara.

As soon as the kids put their heads down, Mara, Kelly, and I left the classroom and crept through the halls.

"First things first," I said. "Scarlet's snowy head. I don't know how she got upstairs, but she did. Come on!"

We followed the work noises.

We saw workmen everywhere.

We saw white dust everywhere.

But we saw fish tanks, easels, puppet theaters, and reading trees nowhere.

"Nothing," I said.

"Again," said Mara.

"Nothing plus nothing is an even bigger nothing," said Kelly. "Unless Brian's right that those kids are beaming stuff to a spaceship, the clues *must* be in that classroom."

I nodded.

Mara nodded.

"That's where we'll solve this mystery," I said.

Now, you might think that while Brian watched the kids nap, nothing could happen.

You would be wrong.

By the time Mara, Kelly, and I returned to the classroom, we found the kids wide awake, Brian fast asleep, and Miss Becker's rocking chair and globe nowhere to be found.

"Brian, how could you?" said Mara.

He blinked his eyes open. "I told you Miss Becker's carpet is as comfy as a dog bed. You can't resist it."

"How do you know what a dog bed is like?" Kelly asked.

Brian beamed. "A Goofball knows everything!"

Kelly growled under her breath. "Except where Miss Becker's chair and globe went to."

Brian nodded. "Right. Except that. Maybe Sparky saw something. Sparky?"

Sparky rolled over on the carpet. "Goof . . . *z-z-z-z!*"

"Great," I said. "We're letting a class of tiny kindergartners ruin the Goofballs!"

We managed to make it to the end of the day without losing either ourselves or anyone else. But when school finally ended, I added up my list of all the stuff we had lost.

It was not a pretty picture.

"Guys," said Kelly. "Miss Becker's going to come back to an empty classroom. The Goofballs have totally failed!"

"F-f-f . . . ," Brian stuttered. "I can't seem to spell that word."

Which proved to me that, even though he might fall asleep on the job, Brian was a Goofball from his toes to his nose.

"That's because Goofballs *don't* fail," I said. "Goofballs *can't* fail. Goofballs *never* fail!"

"We're getting pretty close to it," said Mara.

I shook my head. "Our detective careers started in this room. This room will be the scene of our greatest triumph!"

"But how?" Kelly asked. "And when?"

I began to smile. "What happens between today and tomorrow?"

"The stars come out?" said Mara.

"Skunks wake up?" said Brian.

"Daddy snores?" said Kelly.

"Yes, yes, and I don't know," I said. "Goofballs, the thing that happens between today and tomorrow is . . . *tonight*. And tonight is when we come back to school and solve this mystery!"

7

The Big School Secret

After supper with my parents, I went to my room to change into my snooping clothes. Black shirt, black pants, black sneakers.

I stared in the mirror.

I wasn't a teacher anymore. I was just me.

A Goofball.

And I was facing a case that did not want to be solved.

"Is this the end?" I asked myself. "Have we finally met a mystery we can't solve? Are the great Goofball cases a thing of the past?"

Knock-knock. My dad poked his head in. "Are you talking to yourself, Jeff?"

"No," I said. "I mean, yes. I mean . . . Dad, this is a tough mystery. Stuff is disappearing and we have no clues. The kindergartners know something, but they're outgoofing us at every turn. Miss Becker's coming back in the morning, and so far we've failed."

Dad listened quietly as I told him everything. Then he said, "When I feel bad about something, you know what I do?"

"What?"

"I think of my family. You, your mom, Sparky. Then I realize I can do anything."

I thought about that. "The Goofballs are kind of my family," I said.

"They are," he said.

"Goof!" said Sparky.

"Thanks, Dad," I said. "Sparky, let's trot!"

Twenty minutes later, we all met in the parking lot outside school.

Before anything else, I hugged my Goofball family. They didn't even ask why. Then we started looking for clues like the ace detectives we are.

First of all, the parking lot was empty except for Principal Higgins's blue minivan, a couple of cars that belonged to parents, and one truck that said BOGGS BUILDING COMPANY on it.

The back doors of the truck were open.

"Just tools and buckets of green paint the color of pistachios," said Mara, peeking in. "And orange the color of oranges."

"Mmm," said Brian. "Nuts and fruit."

"Except," said Kelly, "our school doesn't *have* any orange and green paint."

"Aha!" said Mara. "I totally have it!"

"You do?" asked Kelly.

"No," Mara said. "I'm still just practicing."

"That's the spirit," I said. "Now, let's get into school before anyone sees us."

Because Principal Higgins was still at work, the school doors were open.

Inside, the halls were dim, but Brian had thoughtfully taped a flashlight to each shoulder. He flicked them on, put his super nose back on, and sniffed.

"I smell orange paint!" he said.

"The workers are finishing up," Kelly said.

"Which means," said Mara with a smile, "that we'll finally see if any of the missing stuff turned up in Miss B.'s new classroom."

"Great idea," I said. "I'm amazed that your brain can still think after today."

"My brain can't explain it," Mara said.

"Mine probably could," said Brian. "But the government would be mad at me. Come on."

We crept upstairs. Miss Becker's new classroom stood across the hall from the library. Its lights were on. The room was neat and beautiful.

"It's a perfect kindergarten classroom," I said. "But every stick of furniture in it is brand-new."

"Nothing from the old classroom is here," said Kelly. "Now I know how Miss B. feels."

"It's like the past has been wiped away," Mara said. "Everything's been forgotten."

"If we don't solve this case, the Goofballs will be forgotten, too," Brian said. "We will have F-A—"

"Don't spell it!" I said. "Our first Goofball mystery happened in that classroom downstairs. We can't let this mystery be our last. We just can't!"

They all looked at me. Even Sparky.

There was a moment right there in that hallway. I wanted to write it down in my cluebook, but I wasn't sure how.

Finally, I wrote this.

Goofballs forever

"What now?" Mara asked.

I looked through my cluebook. "We go back to Miss Becker's classroom. There's something we're missing."

Two minutes later, we opened her classroom door . . . and screamed.

"We're not missing *some*thing," said Kelly. "We're missing *every*thing!"

The classroom was completely empty!

The only things left were the empty cubbies at the back of the room.

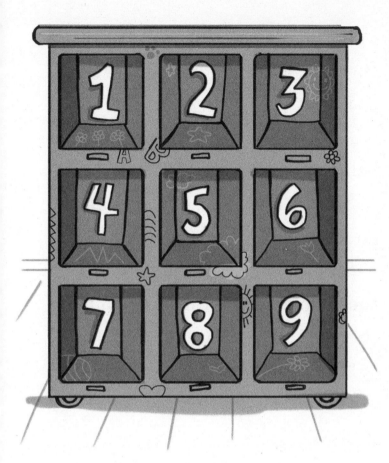

"We've failed!" Mara cried, as
she fell to her knees. "We promised
Miss Becker that we would find her
stuff. But we've failed!"

Brian hung his head. "F . . . A . . .
I . . ."

"Wait!" I said, turning off Brian's shoulder flashlights. "Look over there."

A tiny light was shining out from behind the cubbies.

Sparky crouched, which is hard to do for a dog so low to the ground.

Step by slow step, he approached the cubbies. He sniffed all around them.

"Goof?" he whisper-barked.

"What is it, Sparky?" asked Kelly.

"It could be a trap," said Brian.

He whipped out a ruler, a compass, duct tape, three playing cards, the hook from a wire coat hanger, and a chocolate bar.

With his amazing inventing
fingers, Brian invented an invention
to measure the angle of the
cubby and its distance from the
wall.

He measured it twice. "This isn't
right. . . ."

"I know it isn't," said Mara.
"What's the chocolate bar for?"

"Inspiration!" said Brian, and
he popped it into his mouth as he
measured it a third time. "Now I get
it! Everybody, help me push these
cubbies out of the way."

In fact, Brian didn't really need
our help. The cubbies seemed to
be on brand-new rollers, and they
moved easily and silently aside.

When we slid them away, we saw that where the back of the classroom should be was . . . *no back of the classroom*!

"An escape hatch!" whispered Mara.

All at once, I whipped open my cluebook to the first clues from yesterday afternoon.

"Ha!" I announced. "I bet this leads to the secret elevator room that Scarlet told us her father discovered. Sparky, lead the way!"

"W-A-Y!" said Brian.

We followed Sparky into the hole like train cars following an engine into a tunnel.

When we stood up on the other side, we were nearly blinded by bright orange and green walls!

Kelly gasped. "Where in the world are we?"

"Welcome to Wonderland!" said the tiny and unmistakable voice of Scarlet Boggs.

8

The Goofy Future

Everything was there.

The art easel, the fish tank, the puppet theater, Miss B.'s rocking chair, everything.

All the kids were there, too.

Plus Violet and a couple of parents, who were moving furniture.

We saw Regina and Alison nestled under the reading tree.

They were flipping through a book under its shady leaves. "There's a *the*, and there's a *the*, and there's a *the*," Alison announced.

We saw Lil Mikey spinning the globe and stopping it with his finger any old place, saying, "This is France. And this is France. And this is France —"

"How did you do all of this?" asked Kelly.

The boy named Henri turned from the art easel. "Miss Becker said she'd miss the old classroom. So we saved it in here."

"We took one thing," said Langston. "Then another thing. Pretty soon it was all in here."

"So goofy, yet so awesome!" Brian
said.

Scarlet twirled over to us. "My
daddy found this room last week when
they took out the old elevator. They
were going to close it up, but he saved
it for us."

"I'll be right down," said a low voice.
Mr. Boggs peeked over from some
kind of upper level. He winked at us.
"I'm just heating up my coffee in the
microwave."

"Microwave?" said Mara.

Then I got it. "Scarlet's hot lunch.
And the stairs you used to get to the
microwave!"

"That's right, Mr. Jeff," Scarlet
said.

All at once, there was a scream from the classroom behind us. "Ohhhhh! Nooooo!"

"That's Miss Becker!" Scarlet said, jumping up and down. "She's seen the empty classroom! Everybody hush!"

Two seconds later, Miss Becker crawled through the opening with Principal Higgins, who was still clutching his papers.

"Surprise!" everyone yelled.

"My classroom!" Miss B. said when she looked around. "How in the world . . . ?"

"France!" said Lil Mikey.

"We saved Wonderland as a surprise for you," said Scarlet.

Then she gave her teacher a big hug. "It was my idea, and everyone helped, even parents."

"I don't understand," Miss Becker said.

Scarlet took her hand. "You said you would miss the room when we move upstairs. We didn't want to see you sad. When my daddy found this room, we moved everything in here. So you don't have to miss it. Ever!"

Miss Becker's eyes began to water.

Principal Higgins looked ready to explode or faint or both. "I'm flabbergasted!"

"That's a bad word," said Truman. "I'm telling Miss Kelly."

"You told us it was okay, Principal Higgins," said Scarlet. "You even said Daddy could help."

"I told you *that*?" the principal asked.

"When I gave you my note yesterday morning," she said. "Miss Kelly was there."

Mr. Boggs climbed down some stairs to us. He sorted through the principal's papers and found a yellow piece of construction paper.

"This note?" the principal said. "But I couldn't understand a word of it. Look."

Pins apple?

Misbee lofs r rm.

Kn we kip hrr funnee char

n Wn drr ln nteh noorm?

Dadekn hlip.

Miss Becker frowned. "May I?" She took the note, read it over, and burst out laughing. "I can read this, of course."

Pins apple?

"Principal?"

Misbee lofs r rm.

"Miss B. loves our room."

Kn we kip hrr funnee char

"Can we keep her furniture"

n Wn drr ln nteh noorm?

"and Wonderland in the new room?"

Dadekn hlip.

"Daddy can help."

Principal Higgins frowned a big frown. "And you're saying I *agreed* to this?"

Kelly jumped in. "You did! Principal Higgins, I saw you.

"Yesterday morning you were racing through the hall when Scarlet handed you her note. You frowned. You squinted. You turned the page upside down."

"Well, I couldn't read it," he said.

"But do you remember what you said about it?" said Kelly. "Because I do."

Principal Higgins closed one eye, then the other eye. Then he scratched his chin. Then he shook his head. Then he started to laugh.

"Actually, I *do* remember! I said, 'Wonderful. I love it!'"

"So you *did* agree to it," said Miss Becker. "Well, I love it, too. More than anything!"

"Yay!" the class cheered.

"I'm terribly sorry, Principal Higgins," said Mr. Boggs. "I know Scarlet's writing. When you said you loved her note, I thought you could read it and that it was a good idea. It *does* make sense to empty Miss B.'s old classroom, because we're starting work on it tomorrow."

Principal Higgins laughed and laughed and only stopped laughing to say, "This old elevator room is now Badger Point Elementary's special Wonderland."

The class cheered even louder.

That's when Sparky galloped in, dangling a blue sock and a blue mitten from his mouth.

"Goof! Goof!"

Brian jumped. "Our missing stuff!"

"They were behind the cubbies," said Mr. Boggs.

"The thumb is still switched!" I said.

"So the mystery lives on!" said Brian.

"And so do the Goofballs!" said Mara and Kelly together.

Everyone cheered loudest of all for that.

Proving one thing I always knew.

Goofballs really are forever!